PLAYING

WITH FIRE

FORTUNE TELLERS Club

PLAYING WITH FIRE

DOTTI ENDERLE

2003
Llewellyn Publications
St. Paul, Minnesota 55164-0383, U.S.A.

FIRST EDITION
First printing, 2003

Book design and editing by Kimberly Nightingale
Cover design by Kevin R. Brown
Cover illustration and interior illustrations © 2002 by Matthew
    Archambault

Library of Congress Cataloging-in-Publication Data
(Pending)

ISBN: 0-7387-0340-0

Llewellyn Publications
A Division of Llewellyn Worldwide, Ltd.
P.O. Box 64383, Dept. 0-7387-0340-0
St. Paul, MN 55164-0383, U.S.A.
www.llewellyn.com

Printed in the United States of America

For Dori and Adrienne

Special thanks to Vicki Sansum

Contents

CHAPTER 1

Heads Up!

"Go! Go! Go!" Anne Donovan and the other Avery Middle School cheerleaders jumped and shouted in syncopated rhythm. The gymnasium bleachers looked bare with just a handful of parents and even less students watching the game. So much for school spirit.

The gym was an echo chamber as the volleyball players shouted.

"Get it, Richmond!"

"Hurry, Davis!"

"Go for it, Taylor!"

Anne often wondered why the volleyball team insisted on calling each other by their last names. *It's not like they're all named Ashley or Tiffany,* she thought. But the last name custom certainly fit the style of her best friend, Gena Richmond, the team's top scorer.

Anne's other best friend, Juniper Lynch, was stretched out on the metal bleachers with her ankles crossed and her elbows propped, occasionally yelling, "Way to go, Gena!"

The three girls had been best friends since fourth grade when they discovered a common interest— divination. They call themselves the Fortune Tellers Club, and by using Ouija boards, tarot cards, and tea leaves, they meet to forecast the future.

The volleyball came whizzing through the air and dropped just on the other side of the net. Gena dove for it. The sparse crowd jumped to their feet as Gena slid across the floor, her sneakers squeaking like broken chalk on a blackboard. She managed to get under it with cupped fists, and spiked it straight into the air. The player next to her swatted it over, and that sparked the cheerleaders into another cheer.

Spike it! Spike it!
That's the way we like it!
Over, up, and in your face,
A victory you can't erase.

Admit it! Admit it!
Your team can't seem to hit it.
Wildcats, Wildcats, up the heat.
Wildcats, Wildcats, can't be beat!

Anne was having trouble concentrating on the game, but she put everything she had into the cheer because he was here—right in front of her—Eric Quinn, the hottest guy in school. Eric had just recently transferred to Avery, and even though he'd missed the first few weeks, he still impressed the football coach enough to get a starting position on the Avery Wildcat team.

He sat just three bleachers up from where Anne stood, and she couldn't take her eyes off him. He was slouched forward with elbows on knees, his black hair sweeping his forehead. His eyes were night dark, and when he stared at Anne, she thought his deep piercing glare might burn right through her. But his fiery gaze was offset by a crooked smile and a smattering of freckles on his nose.

Juniper jumped to her feet. "Heads up, Anne!"

Anne ducked as the volleyball zoomed over her head and crashed into the bleachers.

"Nice return," Juniper yelled to the girl who'd missed the hit. "Hey, Anne! Gotta feeling they should rename this place Sleepy Hollow?"

Anne laughed as she smoothed her hair and ice-blue cheer skirt. She looked toward Eric, giving him a bashful smile.

"Stop it," a voice demanded.

Anne turned to see her fellow cheerleader, Beth Wilson, sneering at her. "Stop flirting with him."

Beth had both hands on her hips and gave the order like a true army sergeant.

"What makes you think I'm flirting with him?" Anne said softly. She was worried that Eric might see them arguing.

Beth moved in closer. "I can't read those crystal eyes of yours, but I can sure read your body language. I've never seen you put so much flounce in your flip."

"You're just imagining things," Anne said.

"Am I? I've seen you batting your eyelashes and tossing your hair."

Anne felt the heat rising to her cheeks. It's one thing to flirt, but getting caught at it is another. And if Beth knew, the rest of the squad did too. Beth couldn't keep a secret. It was guaranteed to be in her ear and out her mouth. Nothing was sacred.

"Well, why do you care if I flirt with him or not? It's *my* business."

Beth raised an eyebrow and smirked. "Because he's *my* boyfriend."

She might as well have punched Anne in the gut. "Since when?"

"Since the day he came here and I called dibs on him. Nicole and I are working out a plan to get him to ask me to the Seventh-Grade Dance."

Anne let out a sigh of relief. "So let me get this straight. You have to get your best friend to help you land a guy who you already claim is your boyfriend? What's wrong with this picture?"

Anne envisioned Beth and Nicole giggling and conniving a way to win Eric. No wonder Juniper and Gena called them the Snotty Twins.

She turned back to see Beth already whispering to another squad mate. Oh well. She'd already been caught flirting. Extra flounce in her flip? She might as well give them something to really gossip about. Next time she'd put some extra squiggle in her wiggle.

The gym was beginning to warm up and Anne was feeling a little sticky. Usually the air conditioner was set so low the students referred to the gym as the Avery Arctic. Not this afternoon.

Anne looked up at Eric. He watched the scoreboard intensely. Just looking at him heated things up more. Two could play Beth's game, and Anne intended to win.

The cheer captain called, "Ready! Set!"

> We're hot! We're hot!
> Our team is hot to go!
> You're not! You're not!
> That's why we say—Yo!

> We're hot! We're hot!
> Our team is hot to go!
> You're not! You're—

WHAM! The ball spliced to the left and whacked Beth on the side of her head.

"Ouch!" She grabbed her head and spun around.

Gena stood with her hand over her mouth, eyes wide. She lifted her fingers. "Oops."

Anne and the other cheerleaders huddled around Beth to make sure she was okay.

Nicole Hoffman came rushing down to check on her best friend. She glared at Gena with a look that could melt iron.

Tears and fury sparkled in Beth's eyes. "Gena Richmond, you did that on purpose!"

"Don't flatter me, Beth, I'm not that good of an aim," Gena said.

The coach blew her whistle. "A casualty of volleyball, ladies. Let's keep playing."

Anne looked in the stands. Eric was holding the volleyball and giving Beth an expression of sympathy. This can't be happening. Does he really like Beth? As Beth straightened the scrunchie in her hair, Anne could see her left ear—cherry red from the imprint of the volleyball. That must have stung.

The coach blew her whistle again.

Gena yelled out, "Come on, Quinn, throw us the ball!"

Eric kept his attention on Beth.

"Eric!" Gena shouted. "What are you waiting for, permission from your parents?"

He gave Gena a feverish glare. Then he fired the ball at her with the strength of a quarterback. The sound of her catching it sprang off the walls. Suddenly, there was a loud POP! The caged light on the gym ceiling shattered. An orange flame jetted out, then fizzled. Glass showered down like sparklers. And the kids ran.

Anne, Gena, and Juniper huddled in a corner with several other students. Parents hurried over to shelter their children, while others stood on the bleachers, pointing and awing. Anne looked over at the gym doors. Eric was casually walking out with his hands in his pockets. He seemed unrattled by the whole thing.

"Gena, Juniper," Anne whispered. "We've got to meet tonight."

"Why?" Juniper asked.

Anne stared at the gym door as it closed. "I'm calling an emergency meeting of the Fortune Tellers Club."

CHAPTER 2

Hot Topic

Gena shuffled the tarot cards and sighed. "Is this really necessary?" she asked.

Anne nodded her head. "You know how much this means to me. I can't go another day without knowing whether Eric likes me or not."

"Yes," Gena said, rolling her eyes, "but is it really necessary?"

Juniper scooched in closer. "Just spread the cards."

Gena turned up the first card—the Page of Cups.

"Is that him?" Anne asked.

"I don't think so," Gena answered. "Doesn't a page represent a child or something?"

"Or a new beginning," Juniper added.

"Let's get the book!" Anne was practically on her feet before Juniper grabbed her and pulled her back down.

"No books, remember? Just work with the basic rules. Wands represent goals and ambitions. Swords represent mental activity like studying or worrying. Cups represent emotions, and Pentacles are money or material stuff." Juniper's look was stern. "We'll never be real psychics if we're always thumbing through books for answers. We've got to open up. Trust our first impressions."

Anne wanted to trust her two friends. The three of them had been the Fortune Tellers Club for three years. In the past, she had trusted them with questions about school and cheerleading, but this was different. Matters of the heart always were. "Okay, no books," she agreed. "So turn up the next card."

"Not yet," Juniper said. "We're not through studying this one."

Gena cringed. "Uh—can we not use the S word? I prefer the word *interpret*. It doesn't conjure up images of math tests."

"Whatever," Anne said. "Study, interpret, just get on with it. I'd like to get this reading done before we graduate."

"Look, do you want to know if he likes you or not?" Gena asked, impatience weighing in her voice.

Juniper giggled. "That's a dumb question. Come on, Gena. Eric is the hottest guy in seventh grade."

"The hottest guy in the whole school!" Anne said. And she meant it. Ever since Eric transferred in, she hadn't been able to transfer her mind to anything else. She had to know if she really had a chance with him.

Gena flipped up the next card. Queen of Wands.

"Who's she?" Anne turned the card toward her. "Maybe that's me."

"Ummm . . . " Gena hummed, rubbing her temples. "My third eye says . . . no!"

"Why can't it be me?" Anne was getting agitated.

Gena leaned in closer to the card. "Because . . . because . . . you tell her, Juniper."

Anne slumped. Doesn't Gena ever take anything seriously?

"I can be serious," Gena mumbled.

Anne flinched. "Did I say that out loud?"

"Say what out loud?" Gena asked.

Juniper tapped the card with her finger. "I really don't think the Queen of Wands is you, Anne. I think in this case, you'd be the Queen of Cups."

"Oh yeah," Anne said. "Cups represent love and emotion. Well, I'm definitely in love."

"You barely know the guy!" Gena said. "He only moved here two weeks ago."

Juniper flashed Gena a sly smile. "Did we mention he's cute?"

"Real cute," Anne added.

Gena turned up the next card and slapped it down on the ivory carpet. The Five of Wands. "Ewwwww . . . not good."

The card showed five people battling with huge wands made from tree limbs.

"A confrontation . . . maybe?" Anne said, exhaling the words.

"Are you kidding?" Gena said. "That looks like more than a confrontation. These guys are going at it with baseball bats. Wham! Wham!" Gena swung an imaginary bat.

Juniper spoke up quickly. "It's not physical."

"I know," Anne said. "Wands represent ambition and goals. I think the Queen of Wands is Beth Wilson. She's the one person who will stand in my way. But I really like Eric, and I want him to like me."

Anne thought about the boys at school who did like her. Lots of them. They called her on the phone or tried to sit next to her at lunch. Even Juniper's little brother, Jonathan, admitted having a crush on her once. And some of the guys were really cute. But Eric was different. She was drawn to him somehow. She smiled and waved at him in the halls. She slipped him notes in history class. She even loaned him lunch money last week when he forgot his. And yet, he was just polite to her, not goo-goo-eyed like some of the other boys. Maybe that was the difference. She enjoyed the challenge.

"Okay," Gena said. "After you beat each other with sticks . . ." She flipped the next card. The Tower. "Holy cow!"

Anne panicked for a moment. "This looks real bad."

"Not necessarily," Juniper said, her voice shaky.

"But this is a Major Arcana card," Anne said. "That means it's—uh—major."

The picture on the card showed a tall tower struck by lightning. Flames licked the windows as smoke billowed up. Two people were falling from the tower, their faces contorted with fear.

The girls sat quietly for a moment. Only the soft ticking of Anne's kitty cat clock could be heard among the silence.

"Well?" Anne said. "Tell me *something*."

She'd barely spoken the words when they heard a light rapping on her bedroom door.

"Come in, Mom," Anne said.

Carol Donovan peeked around the door, looking unsure whether or not to enter.

"I'm sorry to interrupt. I just want to put these clothes away." She stepped in, holding some neatly folded laundry, and crossed over to Anne's dresser. The girls stayed quiet.

"Tarot cards?" Mrs. Donovan said with a sweet smile. "Gena, did you lose your retainer again?"

Gena smiled like a Cheshire cat, showing the thin silver bands on her teeth.

"This is more important," Juniper said. "It's about love."

A burning panic lit Anne's face. "Shhhhh!" she said, nudging Juniper's arm.

Mrs. Donovan narrowed her eyes. "Love? Oh, you girls are much too young to be thinking about boys. That's high-school stuff. Enjoy being children for now."

Anne glanced about her room. Her frilly bedspread was covered in teddy bears. Her Madame Alexander dolls stood neatly on the window sills. And Beanie Babies lounged here and there about the room. Maybe one day, she'd stand up to her mom and have the room she really wanted, with weird lamps and posters of rock groups.

The girls pretended to be studying the tarot cards as Mrs. Donovan went about, putting away clothes. "Oh, and Anne," her mom said before leaving, "make sure you get all these Ju-Ju spirits out of here when you're done. I don't want them scratching on my windows tonight."

Juniper and Gena fell into a fit of laughter.

"Mom," Anne said, "we're not conjuring up Ju-Ju spirits."

"Whatever that is," Juniper added.

"Still," her mom said, "make sure you spray some air freshener in here when you're finished. I've got to hurry. I smell my cake burning in the oven." Mrs. Donovan rushed out.

The three girls burst out laughing again. "What the heck is a Ju-Ju spirit?" Juniper asked.

"Who knows?" Anne said, feeling embarrassed. "My mom lives in a different time zone than everyone else."

Juniper looked as though she was trying hard to keep a straight face. "What fragrance of air freshener gets rid of Ju-Ju spirits?"

Anne smiled and shrugged.

"I know," Gena said. "Bubble gum scent."

"Bubble gum scent?" Juniper and Anne said together.

"Yeah. Chews 'em up and spits 'em out."

Anne rolled her eyes while Juniper moaned.

"Okay, if that doesn't work, you could put out kitty litter and keep them as pets," Gena added. "I don't think Ju-Ju spirits are housebroken."

Anne buried her face in her hands and shook her head. Nope, Gena couldn't be serious. Suddenly, she remembered something else and turned to Juniper. "I can't believe you said that to my mother! Never mention love or boys around her. You know how old-fashioned she is."

More than old-fashioned, Anne thought. Old. Anne was never comfortable about her parents being so much older than the other kids' moms and dads. Many times they had been mistaken for her grandparents. Anne loved them, but figured their age had something to do with why they always treated her like a two-year-old and called her their miracle baby.

"I'm sorry," Juniper said. "I wasn't thinking."

"Well let's start thinking about this reading again," Gena said.

The girls concentrated on the cards.

"Okay," Gena began, "here's what I think. Something new has taken place in your life, Anne. Something desirable. But you'll have to fight to keep it. Someone else finds it desirable too." She laid her palm across the Tower card. "Look out. A great change is coming. Not just for you, for all of us. It will flash before us like a fireball, scorching our spirit, and blinding us to the truth. And if we're not careful, we'll be cast out of our protective towers, our lives, never to be the same again."

Juniper's eyes grew big. "Wow, that was eerie, Gena."

"Yeah, wasn't that cool!" Gena said, rubbing her hands together.

"So what about Eric?" Anne asked.

"Oh yeah," Gena said. "According to this reading, he's hot."

Juniper moaned again. "I gotta go. I've got a ton of homework."

Gena stood up. "Me too. And Anne, next time you call an emergency meeting, can it please be a real emergency? This isn't exactly 911 stuff to me."

Gena and Juniper headed out. Anne went into the kitchen to get the air freshener.

CHAPTER 3

The Scoop

The buzz in the school cafeteria was typical for a Friday. Anne sat across from Juniper and Gena. They'd been talking through most of lunch, but Anne barely kept up with what they'd said. Eric Quinn was sitting at the table right behind her.

"So, what about it?" Gena said, stuffing her dirty napkin, sandwich bag, bent straw, empty raisin box, and a candy wrapper into her drained milk carton.

"What about what?" Anne asked.

Juniper sighed. "Are you going with us to the movies tomorrow afternoon or not?"

"Yeah, I'll go," Anne said. "But not early. I need to make out my birthday invitations some-time this weekend."

"That's right," Gena said. "Soon you'll be able to tell us what it's like to be thirteen. Are you inviting a bunch of people?"

"Are you ready for this?" Anne asked, barely able to hold it in. "It took me four hours, but I finally talked my mom into letting me have a boy-girl party."

"No way!" Juniper said.

"Can you believe it? I'm so excited." Anne meant it. She was more than excited. She was ready to turn cartwheels.

Juniper started gathering her empty things too. "I can't go to the movies early, either. I have that audition in the morning."

"Oh yeah," Anne said. "What production is your dance studio doing this year?

"It's a jazzed-up version of *The Nutcracker Suite*. It's going to be fun, but I'm a little nervous. I'm trying out for the lead."

Gena nudged her. "You're the best dancer at your studio. Who could possibly beat you out?"

Juniper slumped. "Nicole Hoffman."

"Uh-oh, she's a good dancer," Anne said. She turned her gaze to the end of the table where Nicole sat with Beth and a couple of other girls. The two were whispering and snickering and covering their mouths.

"She's not as good as you," Gena said. "As a matter of fact, I predict that she'll fall on her rear so many times they'll have to change the name of the production to *The Buttcracker Suite.*"

Anne and Juniper roared with laughter. Anne even snorted, then covered her mouth. Eric was right behind her. Did he hear that? How embarrassing. She tried to turn her head slightly to see what he was up to, but didn't want to be obvious.

Gena leaned across the table toward Anne and whispered, "Go ahead. Turn around and look at him. You've been dying to all during lunch."

"What's he doing?" Anne whispered.

"He's looking at you," Gena said.

"No, seriously."

"Seriously," Juniper said. "He's looking at you."

Anne sat up straight. She knew Juniper wouldn't tease. She wished she were sitting on the other side so she could see. "Why do you think he's looking at me?"

"Maybe he needs to borrow some more money," Gena said.

"Come on, he paid me back."

Gena leaned in. "By the way, you do know that he lives in the same apartment complex as me?"

"Why didn't you tell me before?" Anne asked, throwing her wadded-up napkin at Gena.

"Because I didn't know until yesterday."

"And you're just now telling me!"

"Hey, I didn't think it was an emergency." Gena said. "But he has a great apartment number—1313."

Juniper's eyes grew big. "Spooky."

"It gets spookier," Gena whispered.

Anne and Juniper leaned in even more. Anne hoped that whatever Gena was going to say would be another one of her jokes. She couldn't bear to think there was something wrong with Eric.

"You know why he transferred here and is living in an apartment?"

Anne shook her head.

"His house in Brookhaven burned down. To the ground. Incinerated. Ashes to ashes."

"That's not spooky, that's sad," Juniper said.

"Yes, but there's more." Gena grinned like she knew every secret in the world.

"I heard he set the fire."

"He did not!" Anne said, anger rising in her throat.

Gena nodded. "He went to jail for it."

Juniper laughed. "Oh, he did not. Who told you that load of garbage?"

"Mrs. Dearborn in 1310," Gena said, defensively.

Anne relaxed. "Didn't you say that Mrs. Dearborn made up all her gossip from the soap operas she watches every day?"

"I think she's right this time," Gena said.

"Gena, remember when she thought your dad was a spy from a government agency, and she kept asking you for his secret codes?" Juniper reminded.

Juniper and Gena both looked up, their eyes growing wide. A shadow darkened the table, and Anne sensed someone behind her. She looked back to see Eric smiling down.

"Hey," he said shyly.

"Hey," Anne said back.

An awkward silence followed. They looked at each other for what Anne thought was eternity. She wanted to say something, but her mind was like a sealed vault.

Just as Eric was about to speak, Gena chimed in. "You need something, Eric?"

"Yeah," he said. "I need to talk to Anne."

Anne glanced toward the end of the table to see Beth and Nicole sneering at her.

She looked back at Eric and slowly batted her eyelashes. "Yes?"

"Well," he said, looking uneasily at Juniper and Gena. "I was wondering if you wanted to meet me after practice today, and we could do our homework together."

Gena snickered. "Who does homework on Friday?"

Anne whipped around, threatening Gena with a stare. She was ready to throttle her. Being asked to do homework together was like a date. What she'd been hoping for. If Gena ruins it, she'd never forgive her.

Eric shifted from one foot to the other.

Anne smiled up at him. It was all she could think to do at the moment. "I'd love to do homework with you."

His smile turned into an incredible grin. "So should I come to your house this afternoon?"

A fluster of panic filled her. She didn't think her mom would like her having a boy over, even to do homework. "Maybe we should meet at River Bend Park instead."

"That sounds good," he said. "I could really use some help with that English assignment on *The Call of the Wild*."

Gena butted in again. "Maybe it's because *The Call of the Wild* takes place in the Yukon with snow and ice."

Eric looked confused. "What's that supposed to mean?"

"Aren't you into more blistering temperatures?" Gena asked.

He gazed at Gena, his eyes seeming to grow dark. A vein throbbed in his neck.

"Let's all play nice." Juniper said.

He grabbed his lunch trash, then looked at Anne. "I'll see you at the park this afternoon."

"Hey, I was just kidding!" Juniper cried out as Eric stormed away.

Anne slapped her hands on the table. "Thanks a lot!"

Gena opened her mouth to speak, but then looked to her right. "Uh-oh. We're about to get a friendly visit from the Snotty Twins."

Beth and Nicole were already scooting down the benches, dragging their trays with them.

"What did Eric want?" Beth asked.

Anne fumbled around for an answer. "He had a question about homework."

"Good," Beth said. "Because I wouldn't want you getting any silly ideas, like you were his girlfriend or something."

"No problem, Beth," Gena piped in. "We'll let you stay the champion of silly ideas."

"Don't start this again," Anne said, placing her hands over her ears. She couldn't believe that Gena had become so brave. She used to shy away from Beth Wilson. Now she couldn't wait to push Beth's buttons with some clever or crude remark.

Beth pulled Anne's left hand away from her ear and whispered, "I gotta go." She and Nicole stood up at the same time.

Nicole grinned down at Juniper. "I'll see *you* at auditions in the morning."

Beth grinned at Juniper too. "Break a leg."

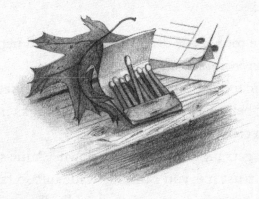

CHAPTER 4

Playing with Matches

The river water hummed at a lazy pace as Anne and Eric found a picnic table nearby. Anne chose the side with the least bird poop and ketchup stains, and blew some dried leaves off. They sat next to each other, spreading their English homework side by side.

Anne was petrified. Her legs and arms were jelly, and her tongue felt heavier than her backpack. She'd had butterflies in her stomach before, but this felt more like a horde of bats.

She took a few deep breaths and told herself, *It's just homework, not a date.*

Eric looked out at the water and grinned. "I can't believe you call this a river. It looks more like a creek."

"It gets bigger a few miles down," Anne said. "But trust me, you can only wade out so far. It gets pretty deep toward the middle. We used to swim here in the summer when I was little."

"It's a nice place," he said. She didn't think he really meant it.

He rubbed his palms together and reached for his pen. "Okay, *The Call of the Wild*. What about this question? The first time Buck steals a piece of bacon it's a sign that . . . ?" He looked at Anne for the answer.

"It's a sign that he's adapting to his environment," she said.

He bent forward and began to write.

"What about you?" she asked.

"What about me?"

She laughed. "Adapting. Do you like Avery?"

"It's okay," he said, obviously more interested in homework than small talk.

"What about the kids at school? There are a lot of girls that think you're real cute." She couldn't believe she'd said that!

"Yeah, I heard," he said, not looking up.

"Like the whole cheer squad," she added, digging herself into an even deeper humiliating hole.

"Yeah, and Beth Wilson," he said with no expression in his voice. "I heard."

Anne felt like she'd been slapped backward. She gathered the nerve to ask, "Do you like Beth?" *Please say no. Please say no. Please say no.*

"She's cute and everything, but I'm here with you." He finally looked at her and smiled. "And you're smart. Now, next assignment question. . . ."

"Wait," Anne said. "We have plenty of time for homework. Tell me about Brookhaven. What did you do there? Did you like the school? Was it a lot different?"

Eric drummed his pen on his paper and looked around. "You know, it's going to get dark soon. We should really get this homework done."

Anne's fluttering bats all crashed to the bottom of her stomach like broken glass. This really wasn't a date. It was just as she'd told herself, only homework.

She didn't know if the hurt inside her showed on her face, but suddenly Eric stopped drumming his pen and relaxed. "I was the quarterback," he said. "At my old school, I mean. I was the quarterback."

"You're the quarterback here," she said. "That's not different."

He looked out on the water, his gaze distant. "Things are never different. You have to make them different."

"Are you working on that?" Anne asked.

He shrugged. "My dad likes me being the star player. He had me playing football from the time I was small enough to sit inside the helmet. We had all the equipment set up in our backyard, and practiced everyday. He played college ball, but bummed his knee, so he never made it to the pros. He says that's my job now."

In the two short weeks Anne had known Eric, she'd never seen him like this. His face looked long and droopy. She wondered if it was football or his dad that made him like this. And she ached to ask him the most important question, but she was afraid. The answer could prove Gena wrong, and assure her that Eric wasn't a criminal. It took all the guts she had, but she asked, "Why did you move?"

He didn't seem rattled by the question at all. "We had to."

Silence. She waited. That was it? We *had* to?

He went back to drumming his pen on the paper and avoiding a look at her.

"Why?" she asked.

"Our house burned down."

That didn't quite answer her question. "Why didn't you just rebuild the house? Didn't you want to stay in Brookhaven?"

"It's complicated," he said. "Like this homework assignment. Next question. Why does Buck disrupt the operation of the sled team?"

"He wanted to become the team's leader," she answered. "Didn't you read the book?"

"Yes, I read the book," he said, writing furiously. "I just thought it'd be fun for us to do our homework together."

She wasn't sure supplying him with the answers was a together thing.

A chill wind picked up and dried leaves rustled across the ground. A few blew into the water and sailed off like a fleet of tiny ships. The sky went from blue to pink. Anne rubbed her arms and shivered. "Once the Sun goes down it cools off quick out here," she said.

"Yeah, that's why we should hurry and finish this." He thumbed through his papers, then opened a copy of the novel.

Anne felt resentful. "Still," she said, "I wish I'd brought a sweater."

"Would you like me to start a campfire?" he asked, without looking up from the book.

Images of a burning house flashed in her mind. Flames. Firefighters. Sirens.

"Of course not!"

He looked up at her and shrugged. "Why not?"

"Because it's dangerous! And—uh—I don't think it's allowed here in the park."

Eric turned around. "Then what are all those heaps of ashes in the bare circles there . . . and there . . . and there? It's only dangerous in the wrong hands."

She couldn't believe it. His house had burn to the ground, possibly because of him, and he wanted to set a fire? Her settling nerves took a turn for the worse.

Eric took a book of matches from his back pocket.

"I—I really don't think it's a good idea," she stuttered.

"Look, there are plenty of dry sticks and leaves laying around. I can have it going in no time. Come on, don't you know anything about fire?"

Anne stumbled for an answer. "My mother wouldn't let me look at the fireplace for very long when I was little. She said if I stared at fire, it would make me wet the bed."

"What?" He laughed out loud.

"My mother is full of old wives' tales. But I'm sure she wouldn't like us having a fire out here." Anne was grasping at anything to get Eric to put the matches away.

She was just inches away from frantic.

He lifted the cover and ripped out a match.

"Really, don't," she said.

Without a word, he lit it, and cupped his left hand around it to block the wind.

"No!" Anne screamed, slapping it from his hand.

The match, still burning, fell onto Anne's homework, and a larger flame shot to life. Her assignment curled into a black scroll, rolling and burning.

"Never knock a match out of someone's hand!" Eric yelled, as they both batted and swatted at the fire. Anne reached down and scooped up two handfuls of dirt and threw it onto her homework. The fire disappeared with a poof.

"Oh that's just great!" Eric said, brushing dirt off his homework questions.

He sighed. "Now I may never get this assignment done. And you know how it is with football, Anne. No pass, no play! I was really counting on you to help me, not burn up the answers." He crammed his stuff into his backpack and then smoothed his hair back with his hand. "Let's forget it. Come on, I'll walk you home."

"That's okay," Anne said, not wanting to take the chance of her mother seeing her with a boy. "You go on."

But more than chancing her mother, Anne didn't want him to see her tears.

"Okay." He shrugged. "See you Monday."

He headed back up the riverbank toward the street.

CHAPTER 5

A Sore Subject

Anne slept in on Saturday, rolling out of bed about ten o'clock. She downed a handful of dry cereal and some orange juice for breakfast, then sat at the computer to make party invitations. She should have been sparkling with excitement, but the homework date with Eric had her feeling dull and deflated. She was starting to wonder if this boy-girl party was really a good idea. She'd be much more relaxed with just girls. But all her friends were inviting boys to their parties now, and she didn't want to be left out of the circle.

She scrolled through the clip art in the computer. The graphics all seemed so cutesy or baby-fied. She wanted something to show she was thirteen—a true teenager. Nothing mature jumped out at her, so she went with a picture of a birthday cake and some balloons.

Before closing out the clip art, she noticed a graphic of a crystal ball. That reminded her of Juniper. She glanced up at the clock. It was nearly noon, and Juniper's audition would be long over. Why hadn't she called with the news?

Anne dialed the phone.

"Hullo," a raspy little voice said.

"Jonathan? Is Juniper there?"

"Yeah."

Anne waited a moment for Juniper to take the phone, then realized she could still hear Jonathan breathing on the other end. "Can I talk to her, please?"

"Sure," he said. "But I don't think she can talk so good."

Now Anne was sorry she'd called. Obviously Juniper didn't get the lead and was terribly upset. Oh well, it *was* her duty to cheer up her best friend.

Juniper picked up the phone. "He-wo."

"Gosh," Anne said. "You sound like you've been to the dentist."

"Worse," Juniper said. "I can barely move my mouth."

"What happened?"

Juniper's breathing sounded ragged as she attempted to speak. "When I woke up this morning my mouth was covered in fever blisters. My lips are just two giant sores."

"Ouch," Anne said. "That sounds painful. What caused them? You haven't been out in the Sun."

"My mom says that they can be brought on by stress. She thinks it's because of the audition."

"Were you really that stressed out over getting the part?"

Juniper let out more shreds of breath. "Not really. I always get a major part in the productions every year. This was just another audition.

Or at least it was until I woke up. It's hard to audition when you look like a freak."

"Well, don't keep me in suspense. Did you go? Did you get the lead?" Anne asked.

"Yes and no," Juniper said.

Anne impatiently bounced up and down. "What's that suppose to mean?"

"I got a lead. Nicole got the part of Clara. I'm dancing the part of the Nutcracker Prince."

Anne wanted to speak, but the words jammed in her throat. Finally, "You're dancing a boy's part?"

Juniper giggled, then let out a low moan. "Oh, it hurts when I laugh. We don't have that many boys at my dance studio. And most of them are pretty young. This really is a big part, and I'll be able to do it as well as any guy."

"But what are you going to do with all that hair of yours?" Anne asked.

"Hide it under a hat."

Anne paused for a moment, not sure what to say. "Well . . . congratulations . . . I guess."

Juniper giggled, then moaned again. "Please don't make me laugh. Okay, now what about you? Are you going to tell me about your date with Eric?"

Anne should have been prepared for that question, but she wasn't. She didn't want to talk about it at all. But this was Juniper, and she knew she had to tell her something. She decided not to hold back. "Gena was right," she said.

"Right about what?" Juniper asked, her words still muffled.

"Right about Eric. His house did burn down."

"Do you think he did it?" Juniper asked.

Anne gave it some thought. She didn't want to believe it. But after the episode with the matches, she didn't know what to believe. "He's really sweet. I don't think he could do something like that."

"Do you still like him? Are you meeting him again soon?"

"He didn't ask me out again," Anne said. "But we'll see what happens."

"Well don't forget," Juniper said. "Mr. Firestarter is also burning a hole in Beth's heart. Nicole told me today that Beth is going to make her big move on him at your party."

"Maybe I shouldn't invite her," Anne said.

"You will," Juniper mumbled. "You two were good friends up until this. Remember, it's me and Gena that she hates."

Anne sighed. "Looks like I'm being added to her enemy list."

"And that list is growing every day!" Juniper said. "Look, I've got to go. Talking hurts way too much."

"So we're not going to the movies this afternoon?" Anne was certain Juniper would say no, and at this point she was really hoping she would. People go to movies to have fun. She still wasn't in a mood to have a good time. Plus, she had to rewrite her charred homework.

"I can't go out in public, Anne. You think I want to be seen like this? I look like a leper! And you should see this white goo my mom is doctoring it with. I look like a leper that's foaming at the mouth! You may not even see me at school on Monday."

"Okay," Anne said. "Take it easy."

"Anne," Juniper said, quickly. "If you and Gena still want to go, I won't mind."

"No," Anne said. "I still have to work on my invitations. Sorry to have made you talk so long while you were in so much pain."

"Yeah, these blisters really burn. And after I hang up, I'm not opening my mouth again until I have to eat lunch . . . through a straw!"

Anne giggled at that and hung up. Poor Juniper. Nothing hurts worse than fever blisters. Anne thought about the cold sores and fever blisters she'd had in the past. Like someone lighting a match to her face. She covered her mouth with her hand and thought again about Eric Quinn.

CHAPTER 6

The Boss

On Monday afternoon, Anne, Juniper, and Gena gathered under the large magnolia tree next to the football field. Although it was early fall, heat and humidity saturated the air, making everything as sticky as gum.

"Don't you have practice?" Gena asked Anne. She nodded her head toward the other cheerleaders gathered by the field.

Anne looked over at them, then back at Gena.

"They're just yakking right now. They'll call me when it's time to start."

Juniper didn't say anything. She'd made it to school today, but Anne felt just awful for her. She'd never seen anything so gross. Juniper's swollen lips were purplish red with oozing welts and sores. She looked like she'd kissed a hornet's nest. And the menthol in the salve that she used smelled like the emergency room at the hospital.

Anne was glad no one had made fun of Juniper. In the four classes they had together, the kids cringed and offered sympathetic words . . . all from a safe distance. All but Beth Wilson, of course. Beth whispered that Juniper had probably caught a rare form of jungle rot by kissing some diseased boy. Anne ignored her and her nasty little lies.

"Do you want us to spread the cards later to see what bad karma brought this on?" Anne asked her.

Juniper looked at Anne with round, hopeless eyes. She shook her head no.

"We could check your horoscope," Anne said. "Maybe this will go away overnight."

Juniper shook her head again, this time looking down at the ground.

Gena leaned in. "Anne and I could pop our lips with rubber bands, then we could tell everyone that we're the Fortune Swellers Club."

Juniper smiled, but quickly covered her mouth in pain.

"Don't you want to go home and lie down?" Anne asked. "You look miserable."

Juniper shook her head again. "I'd be in just as much pain there," she said through the slit in her mouth. "Gena and I are going to work on our Spanish homework. How do you say *fat lip* in Spanish?"

"Or *goopy mess,*" Gena added. "What is that stuff on your mouth?"

"Aloe vera and other stuff," Juniper said. "My mom says it's the best remedy."

Anne giggled. "My mom has another remedy, but you don't want to know what it is."

"I'll try anything," Juniper said.

Anne shook her head. "Not this."

"Come on," Gena urged. "What is it?"

"Your own earwax."

"Ewwwwwwwww!" Juniper grabbed her stomach and Gena made puking noises.

Anne laughed. "I warned you! Some of my mom's old folk remedies are pretty weird."

"It could have been worse," Gena said. "She could have suggested something from up your nose."

Juniper let out a painful snicker. "Gross!"

Anne saw the football players run onto the field and knew that was her cue. "Take it easy," she said, hopping up.

She joined the other cheerleaders who were discussing the previous weekend activities. Susan, the eighth-grade cheer captain, huddled them together. "Okay, girls. We've got a lot to do today."

When they broke the huddle, Anne looked across at Eric. His blue jersey offset the fiery rose of his cheeks. As he passed the football back and forth to the coach, he looked her way and smiled. Her heart did its own cheer.

The girls practiced their routines and helped each other perfect their flip-flops. Anne kept a watch out of the corner of her eye. Occasionally her eyes would meet Eric's, and he'd give her a half smile, and she'd give him a slight wave. Maybe she'd read him wrong on Friday. Maybe it wasn't just homework. She wanted to dance on the bleachers!

The cheerleaders worked on their pyramid and basket-toss, while the football players worked on passing, punting, and tackling. It was a typical after-school practice, until a strange man showed up and sat down on the bleachers. He rested his elbows on his knees and watched the field with grave intensity. Anne had never seen him before, but he looked tall and stout in his green golf shirt and khaki pants. His fingers were fat and stubby like baby sausages, and he occasionally ran them through his thinning hair.

Gena ran over and tapped Anne. "Hey," she whispered.

"We're practicing right now," Beth snapped. "Don't break our concentration."

Gena backed off a moment, then said, "Who promoted you?"

Susan stepped in. "She's right. Can't this wait until we're done?"

"I just want to say one thing," Gena said. "It'll only take a second."

Anne was embarrassed by the whole episode, and wished Gena would just go ahead and say it.

Gena opened her mouth like she was going to speak, then stopped. She glanced at the other cheerleaders. They all stood like statues with hands on hips or arms crossed, waiting to hear what was so urgent. Gena gave them a guilty smile then whispered in Anne's ear. "See that guy sitting on the bleachers?"

Anne nodded.

"That's your future father-in-law."

"What?" Anne said.

"That's Eric's dad." Gena jogged back to the magnolia tree, looking back, and smiling over her shoulder.

Anne leaned around the other cheerleaders, all staring at her, to take another look at the man. He was clapping his hands and yelling out, "That's it, son! Watch your left side!"

"Practice is not over," Susan said.

Anne stepped back into formation. "I'm sorry," she said. "What routine were we about to do?"

Susan shouted, "California Oranges! Ready! Set! Go!"

California oranges, Texas cactus,
We think your team needs a little practice.
Put 'em in a highchair, feed 'em with a spoon.
Come on, Wildcats, kick 'em to the Moon!

★ ★ ★

It seemed no matter how loud the cheerleaders were, Mr. Quinn was louder. "Eric, stay in the pocket! Get rid of that ball fast! You had a man open down field!"

And Eric was no longer smiling, or playing like a star. No wonder. The man was obnoxious. Even the coaches were giving him steely looks. Eric's cool composure had vanished, and instead Anne saw a kid trying his hardest to play his best. Anne wondered why the man bothered shouting all those instructions. It would have been easier to just shout, "Eric, you're doing it all wrong!"

She tried not to look Eric's way. She hated seeing him struggle.

They continued cheer practice in spite of the coach's shrieking whistle, Mr. Quinn's shouts, and the clashing of shoulder pads. Finally, it was time for a water break.

Anne guzzled the water from her squeeze bottle. It cooled the steam on her face and neck. She dabbed her face with a towel, and moved a little closer to the bleachers. Mr. Quinn was now standing at the edge of the field, pointing a nubby finger at Eric and shouting, "Control it, son! Control it!"

Beth sauntered up next to her. "Can you believe this guy? What's his problem?"

Anne wondered the same thing. All the years she took gymnastics and cheer, her parents had been helpful and encouraging. She couldn't have taken these kinds of demands. How did Eric manage it?

"He's a little pushy," she said.

"A little pushy?" Beth said, rolling her eyes. "The guy's a cruel, vicious slave driver!" She took a quick sip of water. "That settles it. When Eric takes me to the Seventh-Grade Dance, I'm getting my parents to drive. I couldn't stand two minutes in a car with this man."

Typical, Anne thought. *Beth was thinking only of herself, not Eric.*

Anne sat on the edge of the bleachers. Even her cotton cheer shorts couldn't keep the Sun-heated metal from stinging her bottom. She hopped up and laid her towel across the seat, then squeezed more water into her mouth, letting it slosh around before swallowing it. She peered out at the scrimmage taking place on the field.

The boys grunted and groaned as they slammed into each other, patches of dark sweat stains on their jerseys. Mr. Quinn's face glowed red from screaming, but he didn't seem bothered by the heat at all.

"Eric!" he hollered. "Watch that follow through or you'll wrench your arm! Do you want to burn out before you get to high school?"

Eric took off his helmet. He turned and faced his father.

Everyone stopped. Anne waited for words, but none came. The silence said plenty. Eric threw his helmet on the ground, and walked back toward the school, passing into the doors between the gym and the library. Everyone watched in a daze.

Tension hung thick, followed by a moment of awkwardness. Even the coaches wouldn't meet anyone's eyes. The quiet drilled into Anne's ears.

She wished someone would say something . . . anything! Then the silence broke as Gena and Juniper ran toward them.

"Fire! Fire! Fire!"

CHAPTER 7

Up in Smoke

Gena and Juniper rushed toward the field, Gena yelling and Juniper flailing her arms. Everyone turned toward the school. Beth stared like a zombie. The other cheerleaders screamed.

Pillars of black smoke streamed through the windows of the school library. The smoke rose like a dark villain, spreading across the courtyard. A loud crash blasted from inside, then flames jumped out all around.

"Eric!" his father yelled, dashing toward the school. Two coaches grabbed him and held him back. "Let me go! My son!" He fought, shoved, and squirmed, trying to push them off.

"He's in the gym," one coach assured him. "He's okay."

With one quick jerk, Mr. Quinn pulled himself from the coaches' grip. "Well, then, stop standing around and call 911!"

Anne stood next to Juniper and Gena, waiting for instruction. The smoke had spread like a black fog across the field. Bits of paper and ash fluttered to the ground. She'd never seen anything like it. Mesmerized, she watched the fire spitting glass from the window. Her heart beat with every flicker of the flames. Then it occurred to her, what if someone was inside the library? She brushed the thought aside. Surely there would have been screams for help.

One of the coaches blew his whistle. "Line up!" Without hesitation, the kids did what they were told. But lining up was noisy and chaotic, and the coach blew the whistle four more times before everyone was led to a safe distance away from the school.

Anne watched the fire burn as sirens sounded in the distance. She thought about the times the Fortune Tellers Club had tried candle gazing. The small candle flame always sat still and calm. But these flames were ferocious monsters, eating away at everything in their path.

"I wanna go home," Gena said, as the firefighters pulled in.

Juniper coughed hard. Anne could swear she saw wisps of smoke poof out. "Are you okay?" she asked Juniper.

"No, I wanna go home," Gena said.

Anne stared at Gena. "I'm not talking to you. I'm talking to Juniper."

"I know," Gena said. "But I still wanna go home. Don't you?"

Juniper coughed again. "I'm thirsty," she said. "Let's go get a Coke before I choke to death."

Anne fidgeted as she watched the heavy spray of water gushing onto the fire. "I don't think we've been dismissed."

"Trust me," Gena said. "They won't miss us."

"But I need to go to the locker room and get my backpack."

Juniper made a weird gagging noise, attempting to giggle. Gena rolled her eyes. "Do you really think they're going to let you go into the school right now? Forget your backpack."

Anne looked down at the ground, then at her friends. "Maybe I'd better ask Susan. After all, she is the cheer captain." Anne didn't want to admit the truth. Like most of the other students standing on the back parking lot, she was intrigued by the action. It's not every day that the school library burned down. And they weren't the only gawkers. People from neighboring houses had come out and joined them in the parking lot to view the excitement. Why would Gena and Juniper want to leave?

Juniper coughed again, and Gena patted her on the back. "Let's go back to my apartment. Are you coming with us?"

Anne looked at the other cheerleaders, huddled together, whimpering. "No, I'd better stay. I'll stop by later."

Juniper and Gena zigzagged through the crowd and disappeared. Anne joined her cheer mates.

"Aren't you afraid?" Beth asked.

"Yes," Anne answered, not really sure what she was supposed to be afraid of.

Tears poured down Beth's face, streaked black from her cheap mascara. "He could be lying in there unconscious right now."

"Eric?" Anne asked.

"Of course, Eric. Those flames hit moments after he walked in. What if he's trapped? Or hurt? Or . . ." She lowered her head into her hands and sobbed.

Anne placed her hand on Beth's shoulder. "Didn't you hear the coach say he's all right? He went into the gym."

"Don't be stupid, Anne," Beth said. "He just said that so Eric's dad wouldn't rush in and get himself killed. How can the coaches know where Eric went?"

"But Eric wouldn't go into the library."

"Don't you even care?" Beth asked.

"Yes," Anne said, feeling her temper rise. "But I'm also realistic. Let's not cry about something until there's something to cry about. You should be concerned about who was in the library when it caught fire. Other kids could have been in there studying."

"Oh, you just don't get it, do you Anne?" Beth stomped away, accidentally tramping on Anne's toes with the heel of her Keds.

Yeah, I get it, Anne thought. *You're afraid you won't have a date for the Seventh-Grade Dance.*

Anne stood for a while and watched the smoke drifting from the library. It was now a light gray mist, signaling the end of the flames. The library, or what was left of it, was a charred gaping mess, oozing dark water—somewhat like Juniper's sores. The back wall had caved in. Blackened furniture, shelves, and computers were all that was left. And those were barely identifiable. Bits of paper from the hundreds of books still hung in the air. Now Anne was glad she'd stayed. She could see the wall between the library and the rest of the school. Untouched. *By some miracle,* Anne thought.

The students didn't wait for further instruction. When the show was over, they scattered, avoiding the muddy field and emergency vehicles. Anne hopped on her bike and pedaled in the direction of Gena's apartment. White smoke followed.

The ride did her some good. She had time to think. Everything happened so quickly. Almost like a flash.

As she headed through the giant gates of the apartment complex, she intended to turn left and ride her bike around the fountain and park it near Gena's front door. But she turned right instead to search out apartment 1313. Beth's crying scene at school came back to her, and she thought it would be best to make sure Eric really was all right, even though she had to venture all the way to the other side of the complex.

The sidewalk curved with twists and turns, and Anne wandered through a maze.

1310 . . . 1312 . . . she was beginning to think 1313 didn't exist. She rounded the corner and saw a small laundry room, and there, just across from it, were the stairs leading up to Eric's apartment. She tiptoed up to the front door, a speech all prepared. She really shouldn't be shy or nervous. She had every right to check up on Eric to see if he was okay. It would be the polite thing to do. But the drapes were open as she approached the apartment, and the inside looked dark and empty. A weird feeling came over her, and she ran back down the stairs before they came home and found her looking in the window.

She didn't breathe until she was safely in front of Gena's door.

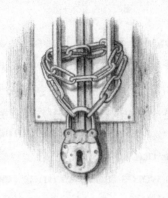

CHAPTER 8

An Unexpected Holiday

"Did you hear?" Gena said, grabbing Anne's arm and pulling her into the apartment. "The fire is the big news. It's on every channel! And guess what . . . no school tomorrow!"

Gena did a happy dance across the room, circling her hands and wiggling her hips.

Anne looked at Juniper who shook her head and shrugged. "Gena likes to celebrate misfortune."

"I'm not celebrating the fire," Gena said. "I'm celebrating the holiday. Now I don't have to do that science handout until tomorrow night. Woo-hoo!"

Anne ignored Gena's hopping about. "Did they say on the news if anyone was hurt?"

"No one," Juniper answered. "Mrs. Thompson had locked up the library and gone for the day. And the fire didn't spread. Smoke got into the hallway, but that's all."

Juniper's words faded as Anne realized something odd. "Uh, Juniper. You're talking normally. You're actually opening your mouth."

"I know," Juniper said. "It's weird. The sores don't hurt at all. Once I got away from the smoke on the school grounds, the pain just went away."

"And they look better too," Anne added. "Have you seen them in the mirror?"

Gena did a hula over to them. "And she didn't even use earwax. But she's right, Juniper. They look more like pink scars than pus-leaking ulcers."

"Ewwwwww," Anne and Juniper said together.

"Thanks for the graphic description," Anne said, holding her stomach.

"You think *that's* gross?" Gena asked. "Did you forget what she looked like an hour ago?"

"Still," Anne said. "Am I the only one who thinks it's odd that your fever blisters healed up so quickly?"

Juniper gave them a faraway look. "It's like the smoke did it."

"Or the water from the fire hoses," Gena added.

"How can the water from the fire hoses cure her blisters?" Anne asked, wondering why she always got suckered in by Gena's stupid remarks.

Gena grinned. "You know, the power of suggestion."

"She might be right," Juniper said. "The blisters weren't just hurting my mouth, my whole body ached too. I was so scared during the fire, but when I saw the firefighters putting it out, it was like the fire was being smothered in me. Everything drained away. Am I making sense?"

"No," Anne said. "But if it makes sense to you, that's all that counts."

Gena clapped her hands and hopped in the air. "And look at the bright side, you have the whole day off tomorrow to totally heal!" She went back to her goofy dancing.

Anne and Juniper looked at each other for a moment. Silence spread between them. Then another question crept into Anne's head. "Did they say what started the fire?"

"That's obvious," Gena said, be-bop-bopping around.

"Will you stop that?" Anne grabbed Gena's arms and held her still. "That's annoying."

"Yeah, it's peeling away at my nerves too," Juniper said. "And what's so obvious?"

Gena raised an eyebrow and gave them a quizzical look. "Who walked by the library just before it went up in blazes?"

"You think Eric did it?" Juniper asked.

Anne felt her insides crashing to her feet. How could Eric have done it? The library was locked. He couldn't have done it, unless he tossed a match through the window. It was impossible. She thought about her homework date with him and his insistence at starting a campfire. He seemed to like fire, in a weird sort of way.

She shut out the thought. "He didn't do it."

"How do you know?" Gena asked.

"He couldn't have," Anne said. "We would have seen it. We were all watching when he went inside."

"Right, but you couldn't see him after he got inside."

"This is ridiculous," Juniper said. "Why would he set the library on fire?"

Gena smirked. "Why would he set his house on fire?"

"We don't know that he really did that," Anne said, feeling defensive.

"Yep," Gena said, nodding her head. "I think he'll go to jail for this one too."

Anne felt dizzy. Gena couldn't be right. "So, you think your crazy neighbor was telling the truth?"

"You can't be wrong 100 percent of the time."

Juniper laughed. "Yeah you can. You prove that daily!"

Anne sighed with relief now that Juniper was turning this whole thing into a joke. That's all it could be—a joke.

"So," Juniper said, "should we call an official meeting of the Fortune Tellers Club? I think we need to get to the bottom of this."

"Me too," Anne agreed.

★　★　★

"So what's our divination of choice?" Gena asked after the girls retreated to her bedroom. She pulled down a night-blue cardboard box, decorated with silver moons and stars. "Cards, dice, Ouija? I even have one of those cellophane fish that curls up in your hand."

"That's for telling what mood you're in," Juniper said. "And I don't need a fish to tell me that you're feeling pretty silly right now."

"I can't help it," Gena said. "Unexpected school holidays have that effect on me."

"It's not a holiday!" Anne snapped. "It's actually a setback. And anyway, we'll probably have to go an extra day this summer to make it up."

Gena grabbed her heart as though Anne had just wounded her. "Why do you always have to bring me back down to Earth?"

Anne looked at Juniper. "What do you think? What's the best way to foresee this one?"

Juniper stared in thought. Anne still couldn't believe how her blisters were healing more and more by the minute.

"Put that stuff away," Juniper said. "I've got a better idea."

Anne waited while Juniper positioned herself, crossing her legs Indian style. "I think we should read the ashes."

"What ashes?" Gena asked, joining the girls in a circle on the floor.

"The ashes from the fire. The true story is there, scattered in the cinders."

"There were a lot of police cars there," Anne said, feeling a little creepy and uncomfortable. "I think they'll run us off."

"We won't go tonight," Juniper assured her. "We'll wait until late tomorrow when no one's around. It's perfect."

"Are you sure it'll be okay?" Gena asked. "I mean, do you really think you're right?"

Juniper smiled. "No one can be wrong 100 percent of the time."

CHAPTER 9

The Reading

Anne still wasn't sure if this was a good idea. The Sun was a pink marshmallow drifting low as the Fortune Tellers Club pedaled their bikes toward the school.

"What if it's surrounded with cops?" Anne shouted over her squeaky bike chain.

"We'll spot them before they spot us," Juniper assured her. "We're not going to get arrested or do anything stupid."

"Right," Gena added. "Fooling around a condemned, burned-out library isn't stupid at all."

Juniper tossed her a look. Miraculously, her fever blisters had completely disappeared. Not even a red spot.

The late September afternoon was warm, but Anne still felt a chill. She sailed on her bike through a nice silent breeze, but it numbed her like ice. And the closer they got to the school, the more she felt the shiver. She doubted it was the temperature that was causing her to tremble.

They rode between two unfenced houses that took them just behind the football field. They stopped suddenly when they could see the back of the school.

"Do you see anyone?" Juniper asked.

"No," Anne and Gena said together.

"But I'm not going to go charging over there," Gena said.

They walked their bikes around the field rather than cutting down the middle. The closer they got, the slower they walked.

"Ewwww," Gena said, wrinkling her nose. "It still stinks."

They stopped at the edge of the bleachers. Anne looked at the charred mess, not believing that yesterday it had been the school library. Besides the back wall, the only boundaries were the yellow tape the police had placed around the gutted area. Some orange cones were in the two corners, and each of the three sides of the tape had wooden barricades with neon red and white stripes. The signs posted on the barricades read: *Danger. Keep out!*

"There's a good side to this," Gena said.

Anne couldn't take her eyes off the scene. "I can't imagine what side that is."

"We won't have to do any more research papers!" Gena beamed like a prize winner.

"First of all," Anne reminded, "The teachers allow Internet research."

Gena slumped. "Www.go-blind-in-front-of-the-computer.com."

"Second of all," Anne continued. "We do have a public library."

"Yep," Juniper said. "And I know how much you love the public library."

Gena grabbed her throat and made choking noises. "All those screaming little toddlers, picking their noses and chewing on books. It's my favorite place!"

Of course, Anne wouldn't admit that it was one of her favorite places. She loved to read. It saddened her that some of her favorite books had been destroyed yesterday in the fire.

Juniper dropped her bike and looked both ways, like a kid sneaking out.

"You can't go in there!" Anne whispered.

"Yeah," Gena said, not bothering to keep her voice down. "Can't you read those signs? Let me spell it out for you, *D-A-N-G-E-R.*"

Juniper looked at them with pinched brows. "I don't think we have to go in. Look at all the ashes that fell past the tape. That's what we're going to read."

Anne was still confused about reading ashes and embers. Was it like reading the shapes in the clouds? "So what are we going to do?"

Juniper didn't answer. She was already close to the library. She motioned the girls over. Anne popped her kickstand, while Gena leaned her bike against the bleachers. They both snuck up to the area. A renewed chill filled Anne.

They squatted down and looked at a pile of ashes that had extended past the tape. It looked like a black hand with wrinkled gray fingers.

"This is the best spot to read because it faces east," Juniper said.

"What does that have to do with anything?" Anne asked.

Juniper looked up at her. Anne could tell she was searching for an answer. Finally Juniper said, "I'm not sure, but I know east is a spiritual direction."

Anne was satisfied with that.

"I wonder how the fire caused this blob?" Gena said. "It looks different than the rest of the ashes. It's darker."

"It's freaky," Juniper said. "That's why I think this will tell us what caused the fire."

The girls heard a noise and all three jumped. It was just a squirrel scampering toward one of the large trees.

"Okay, am I the only one here who needs to change her undies?" Gena said, giggling.

"We're all jumpy," Anne said. "Let's just get on with the reading. What exactly are we looking for?"

"What if we just stare at it for a moment, then say what enters our minds?" Juniper suggested.

Anne and Gena nodded. Anne focused on the heap. It looked like black crust. She was reminded of the time her mom forgot about the pies in the oven. When she finally took them out, a ring of black surrounded a dark gray meringue. The burnt crust overlapped the pie pan and broke into tiny pieces, sprinkling the floor like spilled pepper. But this was more serious than burnt pies.

"Doesn't this large part look like a bridge?" Juniper asked. "See. The black part is a bend, and there's a small space between it and those gray ashes."

Anne tilted her head one way then the other to visualize it. "It does look like a bridge."

"But a bridge to what?" Gena asked.

Juniper looked at them with narrowed eyes. "*To* what? Or *from* what? Maybe this bridge represents a crossing-over for someone."

Anne tried to imagine who would be crossing that bridge. There are lots of different bridges, but they all have one thing in common. Bridges link. Arriving or escaping, the bridge is always a link. But Anne wasn't sure how it linked, and more importantly, who it linked.

"What about these lines of ashes sticking out?" Gena asked. "What can they mean?"

"Roads," Anne said. "I think they're roads."

Gena sat back on her heels and sighed. "So we're not really doing fortune telling, we're reading a map, right?"

Juniper rested her elbows on her knees. "All fortune telling is map reading when you think about it."

"I'd rather not," Gena said. "Let's just think about this. Now, where do these roads go?"

Anne breathed deeply. She planned to give this her best shot. "Look how many branches there are from the bridge. The crosser has a choice to make. Which road should he take?"

Juniper gave her a serious look. "How do you know he hasn't already made the choice?"

Anne shrugged. "Because then there would be only one road. Don't you think?"

Juniper held her finger just an inch above the rubble. "So, the crosser has left something behind, and has all these destinations in front of him."

"I think so," Anne said.

"And do you think he'll set fire to everything on each of these roads?" Gena blurted.

Anne glared. "I haven't seen anything in these ashes to indicate who started this fire. Have you?"

"Hmmmm . . ." Gena said, rubbing her chin. "Doesn't that look like letters right there? The initials E. Q.? And look!" She pointed to more rubble. "There's a jailhouse."

Here we go again, Anne thought. Gena couldn't read these embers fairly, because she's already tried and convicted Eric.

Juniper chimed in before Anne had a chance to say something rude. "Let's look on the other side of the bridge. Where did the crosser come from?"

They leaned in and studied that area. Anne couldn't form a picture in her mind. It didn't look like anything to her. But Gena spoke. "It looks tear-shaped. The crosser came from a sad situation. And look at this small white crescent on this side of the bridge. It looks like a frown. Whoever crossed over brought his sadness with him."

Anne felt that Gena was right. And worse, her words did fit Eric. He left his friends and his life in Brookhaven because of the fire and his father. That had to be a tearful event. Anne reflected on that for a moment, then something caught her eye. Just beneath the bridge was the letter *B*. She dug her finger into the pile of cinders.

"What are you doing?" Juniper squealed. "Don't touch anything."

Anne ignored her and dug through the ash. The bridge collapsed as she pulled something charred and bulky from underneath. They had been reading a fortune mapped out over a book.

"Look," Anne said. "Mrs. Thompson always had a *B* on the spine of books that were biographies.

"Whose biography is it?" Juniper asked.

Anne tried flipping through, but the blackened front cover fell away and the dark pages crumbled like cake. Only the top portion of a single page was still readable. The header for that page read, *Joan of Arc*. Anne held it out.

Juniper took it and said, "We were reading on *Joan of Arc*?"

Gena snickered. "And she was burned at the stake."

Suddenly, low voices drifted from the side of the school. The girls made a run for it. They clumsily grabbed their bikes and raced off through the grass. Anne looked back over her shoulder. A man in dress slacks and a white shirt was standing where they had been, looking down at their collapsed bridge. His shirt sleeves were rolled up, his collar open, and his tie loose. He looked up in their direction. Anne pedaled for her life.

CHAPTER 10

Any Questions?

The next day the school was a beehive of activity. And the buzz was the library fire. Anne heard four different stories on how it had started from kids who weren't even there. And this was before second period!

The morning broadcast came on, and the principal, Mr. Chapman, made a serious announcement. Any student caught crossing, entering, or going anywhere near the fire scene would be suspended. Also, any student with information on the fire should please stop by the office between classes to report it. Then the student council president came on and presented some ideas for raising money to buy books for the new library.

Anne was sick of hearing about the fire. Her primary goal this morning was passing out birthday invitations. The bell rang ending first period, and Anne slid her books off the desk and headed for her next class. Jitters set in as she walked the hall. This was her chance to give Eric his invitation. She was one of the first to reach the classroom, so she stood outside the door and waited. Juniper and Gena walked up, both smiling.

"Do you really think Eric will come to your party?" Juniper asked.

"I bet he's just sizzling to show up," Gena said. She made a silly noise like bacon frying, accidentally sending a spray of spit along with it.

"Stop it," Anne said. "He'll come. Or else I'll be stuck with a bunch of guys there that I'd rather not party with."

Then she saw Eric walking down the hall, dodging the crowd with a quickened pace. His dark shirt highlighted the mystery of his eyes, and his hair fell perfectly across his forehead. Anne's heart melted like ice cream.

"E—Eric," she stammered as he walked up. "Here." She held out the envelope to him. She suddenly wished she hadn't sealed it with a heart sticker. When he took it from her, his warm hand brushed her fingers. Heat stung her face.

"What's this?" he asked. "A birthday invitation?"

"Yeah, my party is Friday night. Think you can come?"

Before he could answer Beth Wilson appeared, one eyebrow cocked higher than the other. She had seen the exchange. "Eric, are you going to the party?"

"Sure," he said, rather shyly. "I'll go."

"Great!" Beth spouted, flinging her hair like an old wet mop. "Nicole and I are coming too! Anne, this is going to be such a great party." She placed her hand on her hip.

Anne wished hard that she'd leave.

"We'll be there, too, you know," Gena added, nodding toward Juniper.

Beth curled her lip. "Can't wait."

Anne wanted to say something quickly to avoid a confrontation.

"I was thinking of bringing my volleyball," Gena said, making a swatting motion toward Beth's head.

Too late.

"Whatever!" Beth snapped. "Just leave your broom at home . . . or is that the only transportation you and Juniper have?"

"Come on," Anne said. "Don't start this."

"I rarely see you without your twin, Beth" Gena said. "Where's Nicole now? Asking the wizard to give you a brain?"

Beth's face turned a furious purple. "Oh, go brush your hair for a change!"

She charged forward to enter the class, but she tripped on Gena's sneaker as she passed. As she took the tumble, a mob of hands reached out to catch her. Eric's arms went around her waist, and after some fancy footwork, managed to keep her off the floor. She straighten up and gave him a smile that sent green shock waves through Anne.

Eric and Beth walked into the class together.

"You're not very nice," he said to Gena as he passed. Beth sneered at her.

"Hey! It was an accident. Really!" Gena stood with her mouth wide open.

"Let's just go in," Anne said. Then the bell rang.

★ ★ ★

Anne shifted in her seat so she could see both the chalkboard and Eric. She didn't want to be obvious, but she could hardly take her eyes off him. He looked so earthy, so natural, so human. Gena was wrong. Eric couldn't possibly have set that fire. But then the incident at the park came back to her, him staring at the match. A chill spiked her, and Anne thought the temperature must have suddenly dropped ten degrees. She jumped when the speaker overhead went BEEEEEEP! A voice came on. "Ms. Weber, would you please send Anne Donovan down to the principal's office?"

The class broke into a unison of "woo-ooo," and Anne sat for moment, not believing she'd heard her name. She'd never been sent to the principal before. Only the rotten kids got sent there . . . the one's getting expelled. Anne remembered the morning announcement and wondered if someone had seen her near the sight yesterday reading the ashes. But then, why didn't they call Gena and Juniper too? A trillion eyes followed her as she got up and crept out the door.

★ ★ ★

She lightly entered the leathery office and stood quietly, looking around at the diplomas framed on the wall. Mr. Chapman finally noticed her. "Anne, you're here." He stepped forward and led her over to his desk.

A man sitting in one of the chairs stood up and turned toward her. Anne recognized him right away.

"Anne, this is Mike Trent," Mr. Chapman said. "He's a detective."

Detective Trent extended his hand. Anne clasped his palm and shook it. It felt cold and clammy like wax. She pulled away quickly. He stared down at her, and she had no doubt he was the man in the white shirt she had seen yesterday when they'd run off.

"I'll be right out here if you need me, Mike," Mr. Chapman said. He left the office door open when he stepped out.

Detective Trent motioned for Anne to sit, and he took the chair beside her. "I'm not just a detective. I'm also an arson investigator. Do you know what that means?"

Anne nodded her head. "You investigate fires."

"Right. And I'm investigating this one." He scratched his nose and inhaled deeply. "I hear you were out on the grounds when the fire occurred. Correct?"

Anne nodded her head again.

"What can you tell me about it?"

She wasn't sure. One minute the library looked fine, the next minute it was in flames. But she didn't think that's what Detective Trent wanted to hear. She shrugged. "It seemed to catch quickly."

"Yes. Yes, it did," Detective Trent said, nodding.

Anne searched his face. "That's all I know."

"Did you see anyone in the library from where you were standing?"

"I didn't really look at the library until the windows were blocked with smoke."

Detective Trent bobbed his head in understanding. "Did you see anyone near the library?"

Anne felt like a fish trapped in a net. She squirmed. Should she tell him about Eric? He's the only one she saw near the library just moments before the blaze. But he couldn't possibly have done it, so why mention it?

"I didn't see anyone suspicious," she said.

Detective Trent propped his arm on the desk, and drummed his fingers. Anne felt he was carefully choosing his next words. "Do you know a boy named Eric Quinn?"

She flinched. "Y—yes."

"Was he by the library yesterday?"

Anne lowered her voice. "He walked by quickly on his way to the gym." She knew that she was there to answer questions, but she had a few she wanted to ask, herself. She mustered up the courage. "Do *you* know Eric Quinn?"

Detective Trent gave Anne a half smile. "Yes."

"You investigated the fire at his old house, didn't you?"

His smile faded.

"Do you think Eric could have started the library fire?" Anne asked, afraid of the answer.

"I don't think anything right now, Anne," he said. "Our investigation is inconclusive at the moment."

Anne sat through an eternity of silence, then Detective Trent dismissed her. On her way out she looked back. "Detective Trent, what caused the fire?"

He shrugged and sighed. "We heard about the electrical problem in the gym last week, so naturally we thought bad wiring was to blame. But we're searching every avenue. Frankly, we're baffled. This fire shows no point of touch-off."

Anne walked out, confused. How could a fire start itself?

CHAPTER 11

The Investigation

Anne, Juniper, and Gena stood under the old magnolia tree waiting for the morning bell to start classes. They could see the burned-out hull that had once been the library. Some cleanup had been done, but the icky smell still hung in the air, and the police tape still outlined the scene.

"I wonder why he asked me about Eric, but he didn't ask either of you?" Anne said.

"He only asked me what I saw," Juniper said. "I told him about seeing the smoke."

Gena nodded her head in agreement. "Same here." She looked pale and seemed unusually quiet.

"But why would he only ask me about Eric?" Anne tried to make sense of it. Detective Trent had questioned a lot of kids yesterday. Had he only mentioned Eric to her?

Juniper shrugged. "Maybe he knows you went to the park with him."

"Yeah," Gena agreed, looking a bit woozy.

"Someone probably told him," Juniper said. "You're seen talking to Eric a lot."

"So are the members of the football team." Anne argued.

Juniper laughed. "But he wouldn't have to ask them if they know Eric. That's pretty obvious. What's not obvious is how the fire started."

"They can't figure it out," Anne said.

Gena shuffled her backpack from one shoulder to the other. Beads of sweat had formed on her forehead, even though it was a fairly cool morning. She breathed heavily.

"Are you okay?" Anne asked.

Gena exhaled a ragged breath. "It's just so hot out here."

"You look sick," Juniper said.

"Thanks for the compliment." She wiped her face with her shirttail.

"No, really," Anne said, touching Gena's forehead. "You're hot. Maybe you should see the nurse."

Gena dropped her backpack and leaned against the tree. "I'm not really sick. It's just a low fever. It'll be gone soon."

"I hope so," Anne said. "You haven't given us your usual opinions this morning. What do you think about all this?"

"You don't want to know what I think," Gena said.

Anne chuckled. "You're probably right, but go ahead."

Gena pushed herself forward, away from the tree and leaned toward Juniper and Anne. "I think Eric is strange. I think he starts the fires without ever striking a match."

"How can he do that?" Juniper asked.

"I don't know," Gena said. "But I think we should check into it before he burns down the whole school."

Anne suddenly wished she hadn't asked. She didn't want Eric to be involved at all. There had to be an explanation. Anne stepped back and studied Gena's face. She knew that look. That sneaky look. And she didn't like it. That's the look that always got them in trouble.

"How are we going to check it out?" Juniper asked.

Gena raised a mischievous eyebrow. "Let's go to his apartment this afternoon and spy on him."

"No," Anne said, shaking her head furiously. "I'm not going to get caught peeking at Eric. Do you know how embarrassing that would be?"

"I don't care," Gena argued. "What if he burns down the apartments? I don't want to be homeless." Her pink face glowed, weepy with fever.

"Are you sure you're up to it?" Juniper asked. "You still look sick."

"I'm up to it," Gena said, dropping back against the tree again.

Anne wanted to scream. Sometimes Gena really ruffled her. "I'm not sure *I'm* up to it," she said. "I'll let you know."

The bell rang and the girls headed toward the side doors.

★ ★ ★

Juniper was already at Gena's apartment when Anne showed up that afternoon. Anne didn't know why she'd even come. She wanted to stay out of it, and pretend everything was okay, but she knew it wasn't. If Detective Trent asked about Eric, then maybe he did have something to do with the library fire. And deep down, she wanted to know the truth.

Gena leaned against the kitchen counter, her face a deep crimson. "Are we ready?"

"Maybe we should do this another time?" Anne suggested. "You look like your fever is worse. Are you sure you can even stand up?"

"I'll live," Gena said. She stood, reached in a drawer full of junk, and pulled out a small pair of folding binoculars. In her other hand she held a glassy, round rock.

"What's that?" Juniper asked, pointing to it.

"It's a mood stone," Gena said. "It changes colors depending on someone's mood. I find it very helpful to know what people are really like."

"But doesn't it only work on the person holding the stone?" Anne asked. "We already know your mood. It's always somewhere between silly and peeved."

"It works by mood transference. It picks up the mood of someone nearby," Gena said with a smirk.

Juniper rolled her eyes. "Let's just go."

★ ★ ★

They cut through the path and rounded the walk to the other side of the complex where Eric lived. There was no confusion this time. Anne and Juniper followed Gena as she marched straight toward his apartment, occasionally wiping her fevered brow with the back of her hand. Anne noticed that they all chose to wear dark colors this afternoon and wondered if it was subconsciously a "spy" thing. Before they reached Eric's apartment, Gena stopped.

"Right here," she said, pointing to a bench inside the laundry room. Gena dragged the bench up to a window that looked straight out to Eric's apartment.

"Now if anyone asks," Gena said, "we're doing laundry."

Juniper looked puzzled. "Why would we do laundry all the way over here when there's a laundry room right by your apartment?"

"Those are full," Gena said.

"But you have a washing machine in your apartment," Anne pointed out.

Gena sighed. "But Eric doesn't know that."

The girls stared out. Anne was thankful that the window was tinted, but she still worried about getting caught.

Gena held out the mood stone in her damp palm. Anne noticed it was an odd amber-green. "What mood is that?" she asked.

Gena clamped it back into her fist. "Jittery."

"Aren't we all," Juniper added.

Gena placed the mood stone on the window sill. "That way it won't be picking up my emotions," she said.

They sat and watched Eric's front door. The drapes were open at the side window, but no activity was taking place. The only noise was the soft tumbling of a dryer.

"It's like watching a movie," Gena said. "We should have brought some popcorn."

Anne let out a nervous laugh. "This is the most boring movie I've ever seen."

"Yeah," Juniper said. "Where's the star?"

The words no sooner escaped her mouth when Eric appeared at the window. The girls flinched and ducked even though he couldn't see them.

"What's he doing?" Juniper whispered.

Gena raised the binoculars and Anne swatted them down. "Don't do that. He might see."

"Why are we whispering?" Gena asked. "The boy's a million miles away. And he can't see through this dark window."

Anne held her stomach to keep it from jumping into her throat.

Gena held out the binoculars. "Look at him, Anne. Can you read his lips?"

Anne wished she could. He appeared to be talking to someone standing behind his front door. "Who's he talking to?" she asked.

Gena took the binoculars away. "I can't tell."

"Let me see," Juniper said, snatching them from Gena.

A pair of slender arms reached around his neck and he leaned in for a hug. Anne's heart sunk. The mood stone changed to royal blue—a blissful happiness. Anne knew it wasn't her mood.

The front door opened and all three of the Fortune Tellers Club slunk down on the bench.

When Anne saw who walked out, she sprung silent tears. Beth Wilson bounced down the stairs with a little too much spring in her step. As she walked by the window, she squinted trying to look in, her smile turning into a scowl. Then walked on by as though seeing nothing.

"Looks like she made her big move," Gena said.

Anne said nothing. She was blinded by the tears stinging her eyes.

"Come on, let's go," Juniper said. "This is more than we needed to know."

As they stood up, Eric's door opened again, and he came jogging out. The girls huddled next to a washer. As he passed, he thumped the window with this fingers.

They waited until it was safe, then started out of the laundry room. Anne could feel the tension smothering her. She knew both Juniper and Gena wanted to say something, but she was glad they didn't. Nothing could ease her right now.

Before they stepped out, Juniper said, "Gena, you forgot your mood stone."

Gena ran over and picked it up, then immediately dropped it to the floor.

"What's wrong?" Juniper asked.

Gena looked up, frightened. "It burned me."

CHAPTER 12

Birthday Wishes

Friday should have been a cheerful day. Anne's birthday. But she couldn't pull herself out of the emotional dumpster. She wished now that she were only having girls at her party. That way, she wouldn't have to face Eric and Beth together. Eric had smiled and talked to her in class today, but Beth only smirked at her, hiding her little secret. Getting through the school day was like pushing a house uphill.

Juniper and Gena arrived thirty minutes early. Along with their gifts, they'd brought their pajamas to spend the night.

"So how did you do it?" Gena asked.

Anne hated it when Gena greeted her with a question. Especially since she wasn't in the mood to answer. "Do what?"

"How did you get your mom to decorate without hearts and teddy bears?"

That question made her smile. "I threatened to conjure more Ju-Ju spirits."

Anne had to admit, her mom had done a great job of decorating. Colorful crepe paper streamers spiraled down from the ceiling, and the floor was covered in large balloons. With the boys there, this would make for one noisy mess. Maybe they'd have a jumping contest later to see who could hop and pop the most balloons. This would probably happen whether she suggested it or not.

"You look like you're feeling better," Anne told Gena. "Is your fever gone?"

"Yeah," Gena said. "And Juniper has a weird theory about it."

Anne looked at Juniper, anxious to hear.

"It's not weird," Juniper said. "It makes sense."

Anne flung her hands up, impatiently. "Well, tell me."

"I think Gena was right about the mood stone. She called it mood transference, but I think she sent her fever into the stone. I bet that's why it burned her."

"Could that really happen?" Anne asked.

"No," Gena said. "I think Eric, the flame-thrower, heated it up when he tapped on the window."

Anne sighed. "You don't really believe that junk about him starting fires without a match, do you?"

"Yep, I even saw a Stephen King movie about it once. This little girl . . ."

Gena was interrupted by the doorbell. Anne held her breath as she opened the door.

"Happy birthday!" Beth and Nicole. They walked in with one big gift. Anne knew they'd chipped in together, as usual. They stepped in, smiling and giggling.

"I'm glad to see your mouth has healed," Nicole said to Juniper. "Last Saturday at the audition, you looked horrible."

Juniper crinkled her face. "Th—thank you . . . I think."

"Are we the first ones here?" Beth asked.

Anne hoped Gena and Juniper wouldn't take that as an insult. "Yes," she answered. "You can set the gift down over there."

Beth and Nicole walked over to the corner of the room where a table was set up for gifts.

"It's officially a party," Gena whispered. "The Snotty Twins have arrived."

The doorbell rang again. A few more girls from school came in, bubbly and ready for a party. Anne answered the door three more times, then Eric arrived. He entered in his own shy way, but he looked majestic. His charcoal gray shirt brought out the outline of his deep eyes, and his cologne tingled in Anne's nose.

She wanted to be mad at him, but he was just too cute.

Soon, the house was full and loud. The boys shouted silly things across the room, imitating teachers, and drop kicking some balloons. Anne tried to keep the music down, but her mom didn't seem to mind. Anne noticed that every time she came into the room, she was snapping her fingers and ditty-bopping across the floor. Anne wanted to hide. Her mom's dance moves were ancient! It looked like Mom was having a better time than she was. But Anne put on that fake cheerleader smile and carried on.

A fast song came on and Stephen Lewis, from fifth period, walked up to Anne. "You wanna dance?"

She didn't, but she had to be polite. They kicked some balloons out of the way and danced. Immediately, others joined in.

Anne should have been paying attention to her dance partner, but she never took her eyes off

Eric. He stood near the corner of the room, drinking a Coke and talking to some of the other guys. She wanted to dance with him, but only when a slow song came on. She moved to the rhythm of her heart rather than the music. Then disaster struck. Beth prissed up to Eric and gave him a little hug. She tilted her head, flung back her shimmering hair, and cozied up to him. Anne's stomach reeled. Nicole stood by her, smiling encouragement. But just then, her mom hurried over and shuffled the two girls away. As they walked by, Anne heard Mom giving them instructions on placing the candles in the cake.

The song ended and Anne walked over to Juniper and Gena. "When did your mom become such good friends with the Snotty Twins?" Gena asked.

Anne shrugged. She was just as puzzled as Gena. "I don't know, but she seemed anxious for them to help out in the kitchen."

A few minutes later, the Snotty Twins emerged from the kitchen and back to the party. But as soon as they started talking to Eric, Mom found another chore for them and scooted them away. Anne couldn't believe it. Maybe her mom wasn't so old-fashioned after all.

The lights dimmed, and Mom, Beth, and Nicole came out of the kitchen. Beth carried the cake, which was actually two cakes on one tray. Mrs. Donovan had made a skinny cake and a ring cake, then sliced the ring cake in half and formed a number 3. So next to the skinny cake, it looked like a 13. Anne was pleased.

"Make a wish," Beth said, setting the cake on a small table.

Gena grinned. "Wish for the boy of your dreams to ask you to the Seventh-Grade Dance."

All the boys oooed, except Eric, who shuffled uncomfortably next to her and stared down at the candle flames. Beth stamped her foot and crossed her arms. But Anne thought that was the perfect wish. She closed her eyes and pictured herself dancing with Eric in the school gym. She took a deep breath, opened her eyes, and—whoosh!

The flames flickered and bent, but not a single one went out. Anne inhaled even deeper, taking in some of Eric's sweet cologne. She blew again. The flames lay flat, but stood right back up and burned brightly.

"Kiss that wish goodbye," Gena said.

Anne was both embarrassed and sad. She believed in wishes and this one had to come true. Then one of the boys said, "Good one, Mrs. Donovan! Trick candles!"

Anne looked up and saw the surprised look on her mother's face. "Well, I didn't do it on purpose," she said. "I must have picked up the wrong box of candles at the store. I'll go check."

By this time all the kids were in fits of laughter, as the flames burned a deep gold, dripping wax all over the icing. They all huffed and puffed, trying to blow them out. And just when they all had given up, Eric leaned over and stared at the candles. His look was intense, like he was challenging them. Then with one quick breath, he blew them out.

Several of the kids chanted in unison an amazed "Woooow!" And Anne's mother returned in a tizzy. "I guess the manufacturer must have switched the candles," she said. "The package says these are just ordinary birthday candles."

Gena nudged Anne and whispered in her ear. "How do you explain that?"

CHAPTER 13

The Village

"It started with a *P*," Gena said the next morning.

Anne exchanged a puzzled look with Juniper. "What started with a *P*?"

"In the Stephen King movie. The *Firestarter* girl had the ability to start fires with her mind. They called it something that started with a *P*."

"Sorry," Juniper said. "I didn't see that movie."

"We could rent it," Anne suggested.

Juniper's eyes lit up. "Or better still, we could take a trip to the Village and look it up!"

Anne pulled up the sleeves of her new birthday pajamas. "You'd look for any excuse to go to the Village."

"You think your mom will take us?" Gena asked, looking as eager as Juniper.

Anne sighed. "I'll ask. But you know her."

★　★　★

"Why do you girls want to spend the day there?" her mom asked. "That place is crowded with hippies. It makes me nervous."

Anne knew this would be a problem. The Village was just a group of new-age shops and health-food cafés, but her mom didn't like the people that hung out there. She considered them weird. They were mostly just college kids.

"We'll avoid the hippies," Juniper said. "We just want to look in some of the shops."

Anne turned on some baby charm. "Please?"

Mom threw her hands up, then grabbed the car keys.

Their favorite shop was called Celestial Spirits, and Anne couldn't get enough of the rosemary scent that bled through the air as they entered. The tinkling of the overhead bell gave off a soft vibration, and harp music settled in her ears. To Anne, it was Camelot.

The place was reverently quiet except for the harp and some wind chimes that sang along to the air conditioner vent. "Let's start over there," Gena said. "In the ESP section. Remember, it starts with a *P*."

The girls thumbed through loads of books, most demonstrating mind reading, the power of suggestion, and developing a psychic sixth sense. Nothing about fire.

"It started with a *P*," Gena said.

"We know!" Anne and Juniper said together.

Anne felt defeated. "There's nothing here." She sunk into herself and looked at the floor. Then her eyes met with a huge book lying flat on the bottom shelf. "Look at this!"

It took all three girls to heave it out onto the floor. The title—*Psychic Encyclopedia*.

"Say that three times fast," Gena said, laughing.

They opened the book to the section marked *P*. A long list of words ran down the page. Each word had a brief paragraph next to it, explaining its definition. Most of the words looked foreign, but Anne recognized some.

Pendulum, pentacle, Philosopher's Stone, poltergeist, possession, premonition, psychism, psychometry.

"Do any of these look like the right word?" she asked Gena.

Gena bobbled her head, looking confused.

"I've got an idea," Juniper said. "Let's look under *F* for Fire."

The girls swung the pages back to *F*, letting the rest drop with a thud. A lot of words filled that page, too, including a picture of a firewalker, and fire as one of the four elements. Gena ran her finger down the page. "Here it is," she said. "*Fire has long been a psychic form of cleansing, used in both ancient and modern spiritual ceremonies.*" She wiggled her finger through the rest of the paragraph, mumbling instead of reading, then rested it on the last sentence. "Here. *See Pyromancy, Pyrokinesis.* That's the word! Pyrokinesis!" She slapped her hand over her mouth when some people looked her way.

They shoved the heavy pages back to the *P*s.

Pyrokinesis—the mental ability over fire. Though pyrokinesis is a controlled skill, some people are unaware of their ability, starting fires sporadically, usually in a heightened emotional state such as anger. Though no one knows why some are born with pyrokinetic capabilities, in ancient times, woman baptized their children in Moon water (water that reflects the Full Moon) to "drown" the pyrokinetic curse.

"So that's the answer," Gena said. "We dunk Eric in Moon water, and you can go to the dance with him without worrying that your clothes will catch fire."

"Yeah, but when's the next Full Moon?" Juniper asked. "He could burn down the whole town before then."

Anne kept quiet. She was still trying to absorb what her friends were saying.

"Come on," Gena said.

They walked up to the man sitting behind the counter, reading. He was wiry and pale and wore a blousy shirt that showed a clump of dark chest hair at the open collar. He looked up from his book, reading glasses still perched on his nose. "Hi."

"Can you tell us when the next Full Moon is?" Gena asked.

The man smiled. "Tomorrow night."

After a length of silence, Juniper said, "How did you know that without looking it up on an astrological calendar or something?"

The man's smile grew bigger. He pointed to a sign by the door.

Harvest Moon Meditation
Sunday night 7:00 P.M.
Astral Gardens
(behind Celestial Spirits)

"Tomorrow night," Gena said.

"Yeah, but how are we going to convince Eric to swim in Moon water?" Juniper asked.

Both girls turned and looked at Anne, and she knew exactly what they were thinking.

CHAPTER 14

Making a Date

"It won't work!" Anne said, taking a bite of her whole-grain mushroom burger.

The girls were having lunch at Food For Thought, a health-food café in the heart of the Village.

"You've got to do it," Juniper said. "Eric is dangerous. And you're the only one with a swimming pool."

"But it won't work," Anne insisted. "My mom was pretty cool last night at the party, but she'd throw ninety-seven fits if I invited a boy to the house. And besides, it's officially fall. My parents already put the tarp over the pool. It won't reflect anything."

Gena lifted her burger, examining it top and bottom. "Where's the grease?"

"Just eat it," Anne said, picking some sprouts off of hers.

Juniper tapped the table, and Anne could see the wheels cranking in her brain. "How about the river?" Juniper said.

"Yeah," Gena added. "You've already met there once."

Anne didn't want to do this. She wasn't even sure it was necessary. But since she couldn't explain the strange happenings over the last couple of weeks, maybe Juniper and Gena were right. Maybe she should do it just as a precaution. "What excuse could I use to get him to meet me at the park?"

Juniper and Gena looked at each other blankly. Juniper shrugged. "Tell him he left something at your house last night."

"I won't lie to him!" Anne said.

"Okay, okay." Juniper held up her hands in surrender.

"I know," Gena said. "Tell him you're doing a science project on pyrokinesis and you need his help."

Juniper giggled. "Or tell him you want to get back at Beth Wilson and you'd like him to give her a hotfoot."

Juniper and Gena both laughed at that. Anne couldn't relax enough to have fun. "I could ask him what to do when you're getting burned by your friends."

"We're not doing this to hurt you," Juniper said. "It's something we *have* to do. Think about what could happen if we just let this go."

"All right," Anne said. "I'll do it. But it seems we're not thinking this thing through. I feel like we're missing something."

"Yeah," Gena said. "Just like this burger is missing a cow."

★ ★ ★

Anne's heart beat fast as she dialed Eric's number that afternoon. "If my mom catches me calling a boy, I'll be grounded until I'm thirty."

"You won't get caught," Juniper assured her.

After two rings, a man answered. "Hello?"

"Eric?" Anne said, feeling her bones turn to mush.

"No, this is his father. Who is this?"

Anne didn't like his tone. She wanted to hang up, but if he had Caller ID, he'd probably call back and tell her mom that someone there was pulling a prank. She'd get caught for sure.

"Oh–uh–I'm Anne Donovan. I had a home-work question for Eric. Is he there?"

Anne tried to ignore Juniper and Gena who were mouthing words at her and giving her a hearty thumbs up.

Mr. Quinn never said a word. After a lifetime of silence, Eric came on the phone. "Anne?"

"Yes." She bit her lip, then gathered some courage. "Could you to meet me at the park late tomorrow?"

"Can we do it tonight instead?" he asked. "My dad and I always practice football on Sunday afternoon."

"No, I can't tonight." Anne felt her face go ice cold. What was she doing? "Can't you meet me tomorrow night after your practice?"

"Okay," he said. "What time?"

"After the Moon comes up," she said softly, then hated herself for sounding like a cheap romance novel.

"How about 7:30?" he suggested.

"That's perfect. I'll see you then." She quickly pushed the End button on her phone and held it to her chest. Nervous air escaped her lungs and she slumped back against the wall.

"He didn't even ask why you wanted to meet him?" Gena asked.

Juniper smiled. "Maybe he really likes you after all."

Anne drooped with sadness. "After tomorrow night he won't."

CHAPTER 15

Moon Water

A nne couldn't believe it was night. The Harvest Moon, nearly as bright as the Sun, lit up everything in its path. The three members of the Fortune Tellers Club headed for the park, ready to take matters in hand.

"Remember," Juniper said. "You get him close to the river, and Gena and I will help push him in. Then you'll be off the hook."

A fall wind had picked up and the recent summer heat had gone. Anne clutched her jacket tighter as a chill forced its way in. "This just seems so cruel," she said. "He's going to freeze in that water."

"It's hardly freezing out here," Gena said. "The worst that can happen is he'll catch a cold. And believe me, I'd feel a lot better about him sneezing after he's cured of pyrokinesis!"

Juniper moaned. "That's a mental image I didn't need!"

As they got closer to the picnic area, Gena and Juniper slipped off behind some trees. But Anne sensed a new problem, she could smell smoke. As she walked down the embankment, she saw Eric squatting near a campfire, warming his hands.

"Noooooooooo!" she yelled, running toward him, flinging her hands. "No fires! No fires!" She dove to her knees and gathered handfuls of dirt, tossing them on the flames.

Eric backed away, looking confused. "What's wrong with you?"

"It has to stop!" She pitched the dirt like a wild person, smothering the flames in a dirty cloud.

"Anne, what's wrong?"

She looked up at him and trembled. "Did you burn down your house?"

"What?"

"Tell me! Did you burn down your house?"

He stared at her with glassy eyes. "Yes."

His answer hit her like a slap on the face. "You burned down your house?"

Eric shoved his hands into his jacket pockets and looked down at the smoke and dust that had once been a fire. "I didn't do it on purpose," he said. "I was mad."

Anne waited to hear more. She wanted to know he was innocent, and that he couldn't really start fires just by thinking about them.

"I wanted to go ice skating with my friends," he continued. "But my dad wouldn't let me. He said I might accidentally fall and break my arm, and I wouldn't be able to play football. I was so mad I wanted to smash something. Then he made me go outside with him to practice. Everytime I threw the ball to him, I tried to hit him. But he managed to catch it over and over. Finally, I threw it with all the strength I had, right at his head. He dodged the ball, and it slammed into the porch light next to the back door. Popped the entire thing apart and left some wires hanging. Anyway, the fire started later that night because of the exposed wires."

Anne shook as she listened to his story. "Couldn't they rebuild your house?"

"They are rebuilding it," Eric said. "But Dad says it was a blessing in disguise and moved us here so I could play football for Avery. He plans to sell the house when it's finished."

Eric looked weak and defeated as he turned toward the river.

"What about the library?" Anne asked. "Did you burn down the library?"

"No!" he shouted, a hurt expression crossing his face. "I didn't burn down the library."

"But what about the candles at my party? You blew them out when no one else could."

Eric shook his head and squinted. "They were fizzling low anyway. They would have gone out on their own in a few seconds." He stared at her a moment more then announced, "I'm going home."

That's when Juniper and Gena attacked. They ran at Eric, ready to tackle him. He stood watching, a surprised look on his face. The girls each grabbed one of his arms and tried pulling him toward the water.

Anne could see the large white Moon floating on the surface. Now if only Juniper and Gena could just push him in.

Eric protested as the two girls tried dragging him to the edge. He dug his heels into the ground and tried to shove the girls away. He twisted and turned, but they continued to push.

The entire scene ran through Anne's mind in fast forward. She needed to help. If Eric broke loose, they'd never get another chance. Maybe he wasn't responsible for the fires, but this was the only way to know for sure.

She ran at him with both hands stiff in front of her. She connected with his chest, and all four went tumbling backward, into the Moon-reflected river.

"You're nuts!" Eric screamed, trying to wiggle his way free. "This water's like ice!"

"Good!" Gena said, splashing water up onto the top of his head. "Don't want to miss a spot."

"This isn't funny!" he yelled, trying to stand up.

Anne didn't think it was funny either. She was so cold she couldn't feel her body. Her blond hair was sticking to her face and neck, but she saw that Juniper and Gena were a couple of wet rats themselves. They all resembled cartoon characters.

"I knew it!" a voice cried.

Anne and the others turned to see Beth, standing on the bank next to the heap of dirt that had once been Eric's campfire.

"You traitor!" she screamed.

At first Anne thought she meant her, but then she realized Beth was directing her anger at Eric.

"How could you do this to me? Especially after I went to your apartment to help you with your homework! You were supposed to take *me* to the Seventh-Grade Dance!"

"Beth, help me!" Eric yelled, still trying to get loose from the Fortune Tellers Club.

"I'll never help you again!" Her face blushed a deep red, and the veins stuck out on her neck. "No pass, no play? Who cares? You're a pig!"

A spark rose from under the dirt, and the campfire glowed a golden orange. Beth stomped her foot and clinched her fists. "Me! It was supposed to be me!"

A blaze shot up and the fire reflamed itself. As Beth ranted and raged, the flames grew.

"It's Beth!" Gena shouted, standing up in the waist-deep water. "It's Beth! She's the one!"

"What?" Juniper said.

Gena trudged toward the bank. "Who was there every time a fire broke out? And your fever blisters, and my fever. Who was always there?

Beth. She was there every time! It's Beth. She's the one with pyrokinesis!"

Juniper looked at Anne, and she knew what to do. The three girls ignored Eric and started toward Beth. But as Beth continued to curse Eric, an ember popped, shooting a large flame that caught the bottom of Beth's jacket. She swatted at it, but the fire spread.

Beth screamed and hopped, trying to take off her burning jacket. Anne thought quickly. "Beth! Stop, drop, and roll! Stop, drop, and roll!"

Beth did. She fell to the ground and rolled—right into the river.

Everyone waded toward her. "Are you hurt?" Juniper asked as she and Anne helped Beth to her feet.

Beth broke into tears. "Yes, yes," she said sobbing.

Anne looked her over. "Where are you burned?"

Beth shook her head. "I'm not hurt from the fire." Then she looked at Eric with pleading eyes. "Why did you ask Nicole to the dance?"

The Fortune Tellers Club whipped around, looking at Eric. Anne was stunned. "You asked Nicole to the dance?"

"Yeah," Eric said, pulling himself out of the water. "She's really nice." He plodded to the bank, water pouring off his clothes. "I'm outta here," he said, shaking his head.

"You're not burned?" Anne asked Beth.

"No." She hung her head. "Just my jacket."

"Come on," Juniper said. "We'll help you get home."

★ ★ ★

On Monday morning, the girls gathered under the old magnolia tree, waiting for the school bell. A crisp wind stung Anne's face. Tightening her jacket, she glanced at the spot that had once been the school library.

"How did you explain your wet clothes to your mom?" Gena asked, smiling.

"I told my mom that I accidentally fell in Anne's pool," Juniper said.

Gena laughed. "I told my dad I was fishing without a pole. The man never believes anything I say anyway." She looked at Anne. "What did you tell your mom?"

Anne smiled. "I tried to sneak in so she wouldn't hear me, but she was waiting for me at the door."

"Oh no!" Juniper said, her eyes showing sympathy. "Did she ground you?"

"That's the weird part. She went and got a towel for me, then asked, 'How was your date with Eric?'"

Gena giggled. "Did you tell her about your moonlight swim?"

"No. Just that it wasn't really a date, and that you were there, and well . . . that I don't really like him anymore."

"What'd she say?" Juniper asked.

"She just grinned and hugged me. She said she hoped things work out better with the next boy I like."

Gena rattled her head. "Your mom said that! What happened? Was she possessed by Ju-Ju spirits?"

Anne beamed. "No. I guess she's just cool after all." Then Anne thought of something else. "I wonder what Beth told her mom."

Juniper shrugged. "We'll probably never know."

Anne thought about the night before. It seemed like a dream now. "So who was it?" she asked. "Eric or Beth?"

"We'll probably never know that either," Juniper said. "But I have a feeling it's all over."

"Me too," Anne said.

Juniper smiled at them. "So I guess the three of us will go to the dance together."

"I'm not going to that dumb dance," Gena said.

"Don't you want to see Beth spitting fire at Nicole the whole night?" Juniper asked.

"No thanks, I've had enough of fire," Gena answered.

"Me too!" Anne added. "By the way, I hear they're trying to come up with fundraisers to supply books for the new library. Maybe we should read tarot cards or something. You know, five dollars a reading. We could donate the money."

"That sounds good," Juniper said. "But do you think we're good enough to read cards for other people?"

The girls gave each other an uncomfortable look. Anne shrugged. "Maybe we should just sell candy instead."

They all laughed as they headed for class.

DOTTI ENDERLE

Dotti Enderle has been telling fortunes since before she was born. She is extremely psychic as she always knows when there is chocolate nearby. She lives in Texas with her husband, two daughters, and a lazy cat named Oliver. Find out more about Dotti and her books at:

www.fortunetellersclub.com

Here's a glimpse of what's ahead in Fortune Tellers Club #3, *The Magic Shades*

CHAPTER 3

Shades of Green

After dinner that night, Gena retreated to her room to read. She stretched out on the bed, her head resting on her arm, and flipped through a fan magazine. Her required reading in English class could wait until the last minute. She started an article called "Rid Zits With H_2O—The Miracles of Drinking Water," but the words just wouldn't soak into her brain cells. After a sentence or two, her gaze would wander to the sunglasses sitting on her night table. *My complexion is beyond hope anyway,* she thought, slapping the magazine shut.

She scooted across the bed and picked them up. Sunglasses . . . just sunglasses. She outlined the frame with her finger. Oddly, the images of Comedy and Tragedy had a different feel. Comedy, smiling up at her with a banana-shaped grin, felt cool to the touch. Tragedy felt warm. Yet the black frame itself kept a constant temperature. Gena looked at herself in the mirrored lenses. The concave image gave her fat cheeks and a beaver face. Ew!

She lay back on her bed, putting the sunglasses on. Shade of green—everywhere. Not St. Patrick's green, not sea green, not even puke green. But the color reminded her of something. Money green? She read once that viewing colors can change your mood. She had never really been a "green" person before, so it seemed odd that this shade of green made her feel sharp, like she was smart, brave . . . perceptive.

She reached in her backpack and pulled out her old sunglasses. They were oval wire frames with brown-tone lenses. She switched glasses, putting those on. Everything looked amber and diluted and blah. Rummaging through a drawer, Gena came up with three more pairs of glasses. One was a pair of pink corrective glasses she'd worn in first grade. She couldn't even stretch them across her face anymore. Another pair were 3D glasses from Disney World. One lens was red, the other blue. They didn't make much of an impact together, but it was fun winking one eye, then the other, and watching the colors of the room change. Then Gena tried on a pair she'd gotten from a Halloween store. The label said Kaleidoscope Glasses. Juniper and Anne had each bought a pair too and had called them Aura Specs. They gave any object she looked at a halo.

She brushed the other glasses aside and went to the dresser mirror with her new pair. She slid them on. Her image reflected from the larger mirror to the lenses, stretching her into infinity. She loved that illusion. Then focusing on her full image, she couldn't imagine why her friends laughed at her. These glasses looked great—they felt great—they . . . *blue-white lightning!* Gena was no longer in her room. She stood in her kitchen, blood everywhere. Blood dripping from the cabinets, splattered on the stove, smeared on the counter. She swallowed a scream. *Blue-white lightning!* She was back at the mirror, ready to faint.

Gena flung the glasses off and clutched the dresser for support. Her stomach dipped like a roller coaster as all feeling drained from her face. She trembled, her knees like water. Trying to catch her breath, she looked at her bedroom door. She had to go out it. She had to check. She had to go into the kitchen.